D. S. - For all the Dans
N.R. - For the staff and pupils of Mithian School,
with thanks

First published in 1997
1 3 5 7 9 10 8 6 4 2

First published in the United Kingdom in 1997 by
Hutchinson Children's Books
Random House UK Limited
20 Vauxhall Bridge Road, London SW1V 2SA

Random House Australia (Pty) Limited
20 Alfred Street, Milsons Point, Sydney
New South Wales 2061, Australia

Random House New Zealand Limited
18 Poland Road, Glenfield
Auckland 10, New Zealand

Random House South Africa (Pty) Limited
PO Box 2263, Rosebank 2121, South Africa

Random House UK Limited Reg. No. 954009

A CIP catalogue record for this book
is available from the British Library

ISBN: 0 09 176532 3

Printed in Hong Kong

UNICORN CITY

DYAN SHELDON
ILLUSTRATED BY NEIL REED

HUTCHINSON
London Sydney Auckland Johannesburg

The first time Dan saw the unicorn, he was staring out the window of his classroom watching the traffic below. He saw a long white tail, plaited with a coloured ribbon, vanish behind a van.

Dan's teacher rapped on her desk. 'Dan,' she said. 'Dan, are you daydreaming again?'

Dan looked up. 'No, Miss,' he said.

Dan's teacher smiled. 'Then perhaps you'd like to tell the class what you were looking at that was more interesting than our lesson.'

Dan pointed to the window. 'There's a unicorn outside,' he told her.

Dan's teacher didn't look out the window. She stopped smiling. 'A unicorn? You saw a unicorn in front of the school?'

'That's right,' said Dan, nodding with excitement. 'It has a long white tail, tied with a coloured ribbon.'

The other children began to laugh. 'Dreamy Dan,' they shouted. 'He sees unicorns in Lupton Road.'

Dan bent his head over his sums.

The second time Dan saw the unicorn, he was sitting on the school bus with his class.

The unicorn was gazing at the road from the window of the video store. It shook its head when it saw Dan.

Dan waved back.

Dan's teacher appeared at his shoulder. 'Who are you waving at, Dan?' she asked.

'The unicorn,' cried Dan, pointing towards the video store. 'It shook its head at me.'

Dan's teacher didn't look back at the video store. She squeezed her lips together. 'The unicorn,' she repeated. 'The unicorn was in the video shop?'

'Dreamy Dan! Dreamy Dan!' chanted the other children. 'He thinks unicorns go shopping in the high street.'

Even the bus driver started to laugh.

The third time Dan saw the unicorn, he was sitting under a tree in the school yard while the children played their games.

The unicorn was on the other side of the playground, eating an apple it had found in the bin. When it saw Dan, the unicorn threw the apple in the air and caught it on its horn.

Dan's teacher blew her whistle. 'Dan! Why aren't you playing with everyone else? What are you doing?'

'I'm watching the unicorn,' Dan called back. He raised his hand. 'It's over there.'

Dan's teacher didn't turn around. 'A unicorn in the playground?' she said sourly.

'That's right!' cried Dan. 'It's juggling an apple.'

The other children had stopped their games and were all watching Dan.

'Dreamy Dan! Dreamy Dan!' they yelled. 'He thinks unicorns come from the circus.'

Dan's teacher blew her whistle again, but no one heard it because they were laughing too much.

When Dan got home from school that afternoon, the unicorn was lying in the forecourt in a pool of grass. It stood up when it saw Dan.

The bells on its mane jangled as it followed him into the lift. 'You can't come in,' said Dan. But the unicorn went in anyway.

Dan and the unicorn got out on the thirteenth floor. 'You can't come in,' Dan told the unicorn as he opened the door to his flat. 'Everyone says that you aren't real.' But the unicorn went in anyway.

All afternoon, Dan waited
for the unicorn to vanish,
but instead it followed
him everywhere he went.

It shared his tea.

It helped him with his
homework.

It watched television with him.

When Dan went to bed, the unicorn went too.
They had wonderful dreams.

The next day, the unicorn walked to school with Dan.

When Dan went to school on his own, he walked through ordinary streets, past ordinary buildings.

But when the unicorn went with him, they walked through an enchanted forest where dragons played and wizards worked spells.

They had just come to the edge of the forest when the school bell rang.

Dan was saying goodbye to the unicorn when his teacher called him in. Dan ran towards the school.

'Come on, Dreamy Dan!' yelled a boy from his class.

'Where's your unicorn?' teased another.

Dan looked back. The unicorn was gone.

Dan spent the morning staring out the window at the dull, grey street. He missed the unicorn.

In the afternoon, it was story time. 'Would anyone like to tell a story today?' asked the teacher.

Dan raised his hand.

Everyone listened as Dan told the class how the unicorn had followed him into the lift. He told them how the bells on its mane jangled and how butterflies danced in the air all around it.

He told them about their wonderful dreams.

No one laughed.

'I can hear them!' shouted one of the children. 'I can hear the bells!'

'Look!' cried another. 'Look over there.'

Suddenly, all the children could see Dan's unicorn. It stood at the top of a narrow path, leading to a forest below. It looked at Dan and flicked its tail.

This time, Dan followed the unicorn... and the rest of the class followed Dan.

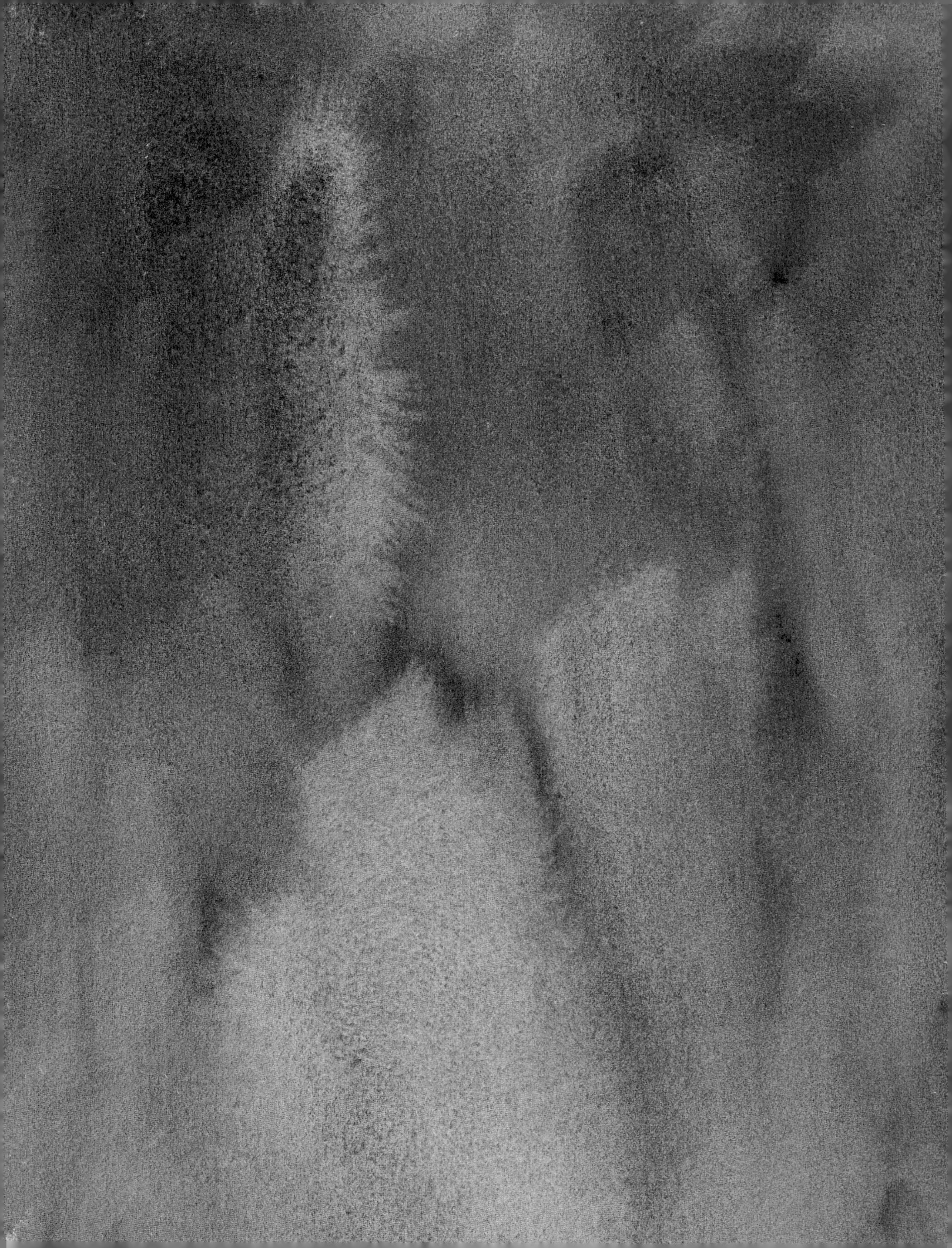